Basketball Stars

Susan Taylor

Contents

Basketball

A Game for Everyone

Basketball is a game that is played by people of all ages. Millions of people play basketball in many countries around the world.

Basketball is played as both a non-professional and a professional sport. Basketball players begin playing as non-professionals for their school or local club. They develop their skills through training and playing games against other schools and clubs.

Players for South Africa and Japan compete in the Men's World Wheelchair Basketball Championship in 2017.

Players compete in a high school basketball game in the USA.

Some basketballers play just for fun, but others may **try out** for a professional league. A league is a group of sports clubs that play against each other for a championship. There are 212 countries around the world that have professional leagues and national teams. One popular league is the NBA (National Basketball Association). This is a league of professional basketball players in the USA.

an NBA game

Basketball Basics

Basketball is played between two teams. There are five players on each team. The game is played on a basketball court with a raised goal, called a basket or hoop, at each end. The aim of each team is to work together to move the ball down the court to the other team's goal, by bouncing or **passing** the ball. One player then shoots the basketball through the basket to score points. Each of the five players on a team has a different job to do to help their side to score.

a neighbourhood basketball game in the Dominican Republic

Basketball Positions

Centre

The centre position is often played by the tallest and strongest team member. Their job is to stay near the basket. They jump up and try to catch the ball after a rebound. This is when the ball bounces off the hoop at the top of the basket. The centre can then try to shoot a basket themselves and score, or pass the ball to a teammate.

Power Forward

The power forward is often the second-tallest player on the team. They need to move quickly and try to stop the players on the other team from scoring. This is called "defending". Power forwards also need to be able to shoot hoops from close to the goal as well as from further away.

Each position in a team plays an important role.

Small Forward

The position of the small forward is often played by a basketballer who is not as tall as the power forward. The small forward shoots hoops and also runs quickly down the court to defend against the players on the other team.

Shooting Guard

The shooting guard needs to be able to run quickly while bouncing the basketball. This is called "dribbling". The shooting guard dribbles the ball down the court and looks for their teammates to quickly pass the ball to. They also need to be able to shoot hoops from far away.

Point Guard

The player who plays the position of point guard needs to think carefully about their whole team. They remember where their coach has said every player should be on the court. They decide when it is good to run slowly or quickly. They also need to know when to pass the ball or shoot it into the basket.

Famous Basketballers

Basketball is a game that many people around the world enjoy watching. Some professional basketball players are admired greatly by their fans. These individual players are seen as heroes, and inspire young basketball players to keep practising their skills.

Liz Cambage

Early Life

Liz Cambage is one of Australia's most famous basketballers. She was born in London in 1991. Her father was from Nigeria and her mother was from Australia. Liz and her mother moved back to Australia when Liz was a baby. At first, they lived in Eden, New South Wales. When Liz was ten years old, the family moved to Melbourne. Liz was already six feet (183 centimetres) tall at this age. Her mother suggested that she play basketball so she could meet new people and make friends.

Learning the Game

Liz joined the Australian Institute of Sport (a place for talented athletes) in 2007 so she could focus on developing her basketball skills. In 2009, she was selected to join the Opals – the Australian women's basketball team. Liz also played in the Australian Women's National Basketball League (WNBL) for the Bulleen Boomers. She helped them to win the WNBL Championship in 2011.

Liz was awarded a **scholarship** in 2011 by the Sports Australia Hall of Fame. This meant Liz had a **mentor**, Sue Stanley, who had been a high-level athlete herself. Sue helped Liz with her basketball career by guiding, motivating and encouraging her.

When Liz Cambage is not playing basketball, she enjoys listening to music with her friends.

Liz Cambage (right) plays for Australia against Brazil.

On the Court

Liz Cambage played centre in her teams. This position suited Liz, who was a tall and confident player.

From 2011 to 2013, Liz played for the Tulsa Shock, a Women's National Basketball Association (WNBA) team in the USA. Then, from 2013 to 2016, Liz played in China in the Women's Chinese Basketball Association (WCBA).

From 2017 to 2021, Liz played basketball in the national leagues in both Australia and the USA. She represented Australia at the 2012 London Olympics, where she helped the Opals to win a bronze medal. Liz also played for Australia in the 2016 Rio de Janeiro Olympics.

Liz Cambage plays for Tulsa Shock against Seattle Storm in 2011.

Achievements

Liz Cambage was named the Australian WNBL "Player of the Week" on six separate occasions. In the USA, she received the WNBA All-Star award in 2011, 2018 and 2019.

Liz holds the WNBA record for the most points scored in a single game for her performance in New York on 17 July 2018, when she scored 53 points. She was also the first female player to **slam dunk** in an Olympic competition, in the 2012 London Olympics.

Liz Cambage plays for Australia against Brazil in 2012.

Patty Mills

Early Life

Patty Mills is another famous Australian basketball player. He was born in Canberra in 1988. Patty Mills is a First Nations Australian. His mother, Yvonne Mills, is an Aboriginal Australian from the Kokatha people and his father, Benny Mills, is a Torres Strait Islander from the Muralag people.

Patty Mills (left) played for the St Mary's College basketball team.

Learning the Game

Patty Mills began playing basketball when he was four years old. As a child, he played for a First Nations team his parents formed, called The Shadows.

Patty Mills' uncle, Danny Morseu, was a former Olympic basketball player. Danny Morseu encouraged Patty Mills to play basketball. Patty Mills was also a ball boy for the Canberra Cannons. This meant he collected the basketball if it went off the court while the Cannons were playing.

During this time, Patty Mills met David Patrick, a player for the Canberra Cannons, who became his mentor. David later became Patty Mills' coach when Patty Mills played for the St Mary's College basketball team in the USA in 2009.

Patty Mills (left) at age 19 with his uncle Danny Morseu

On the Court

Well known for his three-point shooting, Patty Mills has played in the point guard position in various leagues around the world. He has played for several NBA teams in the USA including the Portland Trail Blazers, the San Antonio Spurs and the Brooklyn Nets. He has also belonged to the Melbourne Tigers, a team in Australia's National Basketball League (NBL).

Achievements

Patty Mills was the youngest Australian player to compete in the Olympic Games in basketball. He was 20 years old when he played a key role in the Australian Boomers' matches in the 2008 Beijing Olympics. Patty Mills also competed in the 2012 London Olympics and the 2016 Rio de Janeiro Olympics.

In the Tokyo Olympics, held in 2021, Patty Mills scored 42 points as captain of the Boomers and helped Australia to win their first ever Olympic medal in men's basketball. He was also the first First Nations Australian to be a **flag bearer** in the opening ceremony of an Olympic Games.

Patty Mills began a **trend** called the "Three Goggles" hand signal. His teammate in the Portland Trail Blazers, Rudy Fernandez, couldn't see very well and was worried about shooting baskets from far away. Patty Mills would make the goggles shape over his eyes to celebrate when Rudy successfully made a three-point shot.

Patty Mills (right) plays for Australia against France in 2019.

Steven Adams

Early Life

Steven Funaki Adams is a famous basketball player from New Zealand. He was born in Rotorua, New Zealand, in 1993. His father, Sid Adams, was from England and his mother, Lilika Ngauamo, was from the Pacific island of Tonga.

Steven Adams moved to Wellington as a teenager. While he was in Wellington, his older brother, Warren Adams, encouraged his interest in basketball. Warren Adams had played basketball for the New Zealand national team.

Steven Adams has 17 brothers and sisters. Six of his siblings play basketball for New Zealand. One of Steven Adams's sisters is a Paralympic athlete, and another sister is an Olympic athlete.

Steven Adams plays for the Memphis Grizzlies in 2022.

Steven Adams plays for the Oklahoma City Thunder in 2019.

Learning the Game

In Wellington, Steven Adams was introduced to Kenny McFadden, a basketball coach, who became his mentor. Kenny invited Steven Adams to join a basketball **academy** where he could work on his skills in basketball. He also helped Steven Adams to gain a scholarship to Scots College, a private school in Wellington. Steven Adams was able to develop his basketball skills while he was at Scots College.

On the Court

In 2011, Steven Adams played for the Wellington Saints, and helped them to win the New Zealand National Basketball League (NZNBL) Championship. He won a basketball scholarship to the University of Pittsburgh, in the USA, in 2012. From 2013 onwards, Steven Adams played for three different NBA teams in the USA: the Oklahoma City Thunder, the New Orleans Pelicans and the Memphis Grizzlies. Steven Adams played in the centre position and was known for being physically strong. He was also very skilled at catching rebounds from the basket.

Achievements

Steven Adams won the NZNBL's Rookie of the Year Award in 2011 in New Zealand. A "rookie" is a new player in their first season in the league.

In 2013, Steven Adams was chosen to join the NBA in the USA. This was the first time a basketball player from New Zealand was chosen, ahead of so many other players.

Steven Adams (right) plays for the Oklahoma City Thunder in 2018.

Patrick Anderson

Early Life

Patrick Anderson is a highly respected wheelchair basketball player. Wheelchair basketball is a difficult game because it is a fast-paced **contact sport**. Players need to be able to move and turn their wheelchair quickly to avoid the players on the opposing team and to keep control of the ball.

Patrick was born in Edmonton, Canada, in 1979 and spent most of his early childhood in the riverside town of Fergus. Patrick grew up playing many sports, including ice hockey.

At the age of nine, Patrick was in a serious car accident and had to have both legs **amputated** below the knee. After the accident, Patrick had to learn to use a wheelchair. He was determined to use his athletic ability to play sport. In 1990, he began to play wheelchair basketball.

Patrick Anderson plays for Canada at the 2011 Paralympic World Cup.

Learning the Game

Patrick trained hard, and in 1997 he was selected for the Canadian national wheelchair basketball team. This meant he would go on to represent his country at the Paralympic Games. Patrick also won a scholarship to study and play wheelchair basketball at the University of Illinois in the USA.

Patrick was a member of the Canadian Junior Men's national team. He led the team to victory at the World Championships in 1997 and again in 2001. Patrick's talent on the court was noticed by **officials** at the championships. He was named the most valuable player (MVP) both times.

Patrick Anderson (front right) plays for Canada at the 2020 Paralympic Games in Tokyo.

On the Court

Patrick has competed in professional leagues in the USA, Germany, Australia and Turkey. He has competed in five Paralympic Games, where he won three gold medals and one silver medal. Patrick is best known for his speed and flair on the court. He has worked hard to develop his skills in these important areas.

Achievements

Patrick Anderson is widely considered to be the greatest wheelchair basketball player of all time. He was given the title of "mayor of the Olympic and Paralympic Games" in the 2010 Vancouver Winter Olympics. In 2018, Patrick received the Wheelchair Basketball Canada Male Athlete of the Year Award.

Patrick learned to juggle when he was six years of age. He often juggles before he plays a game of basketball. This helps him to get his mind and hands ready for the game.

Patrick Anderson plays for Canada in the 2012 Paralympic Games in London.

LeBron James

Early Life

LeBron James (nicknamed "King James") is an American basketball star. He was born in 1984 in Akron, Ohio, in the USA. LeBron grew up in a poor family. He lived in many different houses and attended several schools during his childhood.

LeBron's mother, Gloria, said that he was interested in basketball from the age of two. She noticed this when she bought him a plastic basketball stand as a Christmas present.

LeBron James plays for St Vincent–St Mary High School in 2003.

Learning the Game

LeBron James was introduced to the game of basketball by Frank Walker, who was originally his football coach in a local team, the South Side Rangers. Frank was supportive of LeBron's early basketball career.

LeBron had three close childhood friends, Sian Cotton, Willie McGee and Dru Joyce the Third. They were basketball teammates who called themselves "The Fab Four". LeBron and his friends attended St Vincent–St Mary High School, as this was a school with a good basketball program. Here, LeBron and his friends played for the school's basketball team, the Fighting Irish. The team made history by winning three state championships and a national title while LeBron and his friends were on it.

LeBron James (left) with the rest of "The Fab Four" in 2000

LeBron James performs a slam dunk in a game in 2003, playing for the Cleveland Cavaliers.

On the Court

LeBron James was known as a basketballer who played many positions well. At different times, he played shooting guard, small forward, power forward and point guard in the NBA. From 2003 to 2018, LeBron played for the Cleveland Cavaliers, the Miami Heat and the Los Angeles Lakers teams.

LeBron played basketball for the USA team at the 2004 Athens Olympics, then at the 2008 Beijing Olympics and again at the 2012 London Olympics. His team won two gold medals and one bronze medal.

Achievements

When LeBron was 20 years old, he made history by becoming the first member of the Cleveland Cavaliers to win NBA Rookie of the Year. LeBron was selected as the NBA's MVP four times, from 2008 to 2013. He was named in the NBA's All-Defensive Team, an honour given to the best defensive players each year, six times from 2009 to 2014.

LeBron starred with the cartoon character Bugs Bunny in the 2021 movie ***Space Jam: A New Legacy***. This was a sequel to the 1996 movie ***Space Jam***, starring another famous basketball player, Michael Jordan.

Michael Jordan

Early Life

Michael Jordan (nicknamed "MJ") is one of the most famous basketball players in the world. Although Michael no longer plays, he still has many fans. Michael was born in 1963 in Brooklyn, New York, in the USA. When Michael was five years old, his family moved to Wilmington, North Carolina. Michael's father, James, built a basketball court for Michael in their backyard.

Michael attended Emsley A. Laney High School. While he was at high school, Michael played baseball and football as well as basketball.

Learning the Game

Michael's talents were noticed in a high school basketball game by a coach called Dean Smith. Dean was the basketball coach at the University of North Carolina, and he selected Michael to play there after high school. This was an incredible achievement.

During his time at the university, Michael performed a difficult shot that he became famous for. In a 1982 college championship game, Michael made a "jump shot" that won his team the game. A jump shot is when a player throws the ball at the hoop with one hand while jumping.

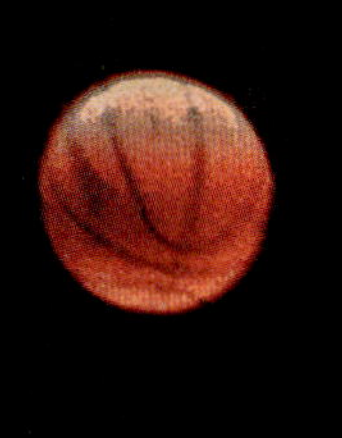

Michael Jordan performs a jump shot in 1985, playing for the Chicago Bulls.

On the Court

Michael Jordan played shooting guard for the Chicago Bulls (an NBA team) from 1984 to 1998.

Michael also played for another NBA team, the Washington Wizards, from 2001 to 2003. He won gold medals playing for the USA basketball team in the 1984 Los Angeles Olympics and the 1992 Barcelona Olympics. Michael Jordan remains famous for his incredible **athleticism** on the court, particularly his ability to perform slam dunks.

Achievements

Michael Jordan received the most awards in NBA history at the time he was playing. He received the MVP award from the NBA five times from 1988 to 1998. He was the captain of the Chicago Bulls in six NBA Championships.

In 2016, US President Barack Obama presented Michael with the highest honour, the Presidential Medal of Freedom.

LeBron James takes a selfie with a fan in 2015.

Basketball is a game played by many people in different countries around the world. Basketball players begin as non-professional players. Some develop their basketball skills so they can become professional players. Professional basketball players have many fans and are seen as inspiring heroes to young players.

Glossary

academy (*noun*)	a place to study or train
amputated (*verb*)	to be cut off by doctors (e.g. a leg)
athleticism (*noun*)	the qualities that make someone a good athlete, such as speed and fitness
contact sport (*noun*)	a sport where players need to touch or bump into each other as they play
flag bearer (*noun*)	the athlete from each country who has the honour of carrying the country's flag in the opening ceremony of an Olympic Games
mentor (*noun*)	somebody with more experience who gives a young person advice as they learn their skills
officials (*noun*)	people whose job is to make decisions at events like basketball games
passing (*verb*)	throwing the ball to someone else on your team
scholarship (*noun*)	money or other resources awarded to someone to help them while they study or train
slam dunk (*verb*)	to jump up and push the ball down through the net with your hand
trend (*noun*)	something that many people start to do
try out (*verb*)	to compete for a place on a sports team